Working for Her Dad's Best Friend

Alyse Zaftig

ISBN-13: 9781520464732

D1475145

Fantasy

Camilla

My eyes are glazing over as I sort through the never-ending ton of emails that are coming for my boss. Anybody who knows his actual email address emails him directly, but I handle his publicly available email address. About 90% of the emails are crazy, but I pass on maybe 10%. It works for him. It's a part-time job for me.

I come to work after class each day, dressed in business professional and wading through a torrent of emails. I want to quit though, because I can't stop fantasizing about my boss, Lincoln.

He has dark hair with a handful of silver streaks running through it, but his hair only enhances how gorgeous he is. He's my dad's best friend, so he's always been around.

And I've always had a crush on him.

Today, the amazing gray suit that he's wearing fits him perfectly, like all of his suits. They're tailored specifically for him. He can't buy off the rack, with his linebacker shoulders and slender waist. He looks like a model and did a little modeling in college for spare money, before he founded his own software company. He and my dad love to go out on the weekend, go into the mountains, and totally unplug. I've been along a few times, but it's hard to sleep in a tent only a few feet away from him and my dad.

It's crazy that someone afraid that she'll show her feelings actually is working for her crush, but that's how it happened. I needed a summer job. His secretary, Amanda, was on maternity leave. My dad thought it was a perfect fit.

So now I'm stuck in an unending hell, fantasizing about a man I can never have.

* * *

"Come into my office." Lincoln is so tall that I have to tilt back my head to look up at him.

"Coming, sir." I straighten my skirt, smoothing it down my thighs. It rode up while I was sitting, almost exposing a little too much.

When I step into his office, he tells me, "Close the door."

I turn to close it. Then I feel his big body behind me, his heat searing my skin even through our clothes. His cock is pressing into my lower back.

"I'm tired of you teasing me," he whispers softly. "So you're going to get what you've been asking for."

We both hear the soft sound of my zipper going down, down, down, just a millimeter at a time. My heart is pounding like a drum. My body is crushed between the wood door and his hard body. I can feel his erection pulse once behind me.

Stepping back, he pushes my skirt off of my hips.

"Step out of it," he commands.

I step out of it. I'm still wearing my blouse, a bra, a black lace thong, and heels.

He snaps the waistband of my thong.

"Take this off."

All of this is so inappropriate. "I don't think..."

"Don't think. Do as you're told." His hand spanks my right cheek. "Now."

With shaking hands, I pull off my thong. Now my top half is covered, but my bottom half is bare.

I can hear a thud as something hits the ground. His hands are pulling my ass cheeks apart. Then I feel a tongue between my legs.

"Oh my god," I gasp.

"Be quiet," he says. "Don't make a sound."

I can feel his tongue enter me again. My lower body is melting. I don't know if I can be quiet.

His hand is now touching my clit, rubbing it over and over as his tongue is still inside of my folds. My legs are shaking and no longer able to hold me up.

"Link," I whisper.

He slaps my ass again, but he hits harder this time. "I told you to be quiet. I guess I need to gag you."

I hear some soft sounds before he's shoving his tie into my mouth.

"Mmph!" I protest.

He bites my ear. "I can take it out. I can take it out right now. You can take your skirt and go right back to your desk. Or I can make you come. Make another sound, and I'll send you away, wet or not."

I'm quiet.

"That's what I thought."

Closing Time

Lincoln

"Camilla."

Her beautiful brown eyes go up to meet mine. Her face flushes a little.

"Yes, sir. What can I do for you?"

"It's time to go home." I point at the clock. "Everyone left a half hour ago. It's just you and me. You should get home, or I'll have to have a talk with your dad about appropriate work-life balance."

"Right away." Her face is still flushed.

I watch as she bends over to get her backpack. She's a good girl. I know that she comes here straight from the summer classes she's taking at a local community college. My buddy wants to teach her about responsibility and the value of a dollar, so even though he's perfectly capable of providing for her, he makes her work during the summer to pad her resume.

It's been sheer hell. She always wears these tight skirts that emphasize the curve of her hips, especially when she's bent over like she is now. I've spent this summer adjusting my erection because it's so inappropriate for me to feel this way about my temporary secretary. When my normal secretary, Amanda, told me that she was knocked up and taking advantage of the standard three months of maternity leave, I was panicking. But my buddy Jack said to give his little girl a job, and here we are. I'm staring at her red skirt pulling tight against her ass while she throws things into her bag. There aren't any visible panty lines, which means that she's wearing a thong or going bare.

The thought of Camilla going bare makes me harder than ever. If I don't stop staring at her curvy ass, I'm going to drip some pre-come.

Then she's standing up and sliding her backpack on her shoulders. "I'm going home. I'll see you tomorrow."

"See you tomorrow."

I watch as she walks to the elevators. Her curly hair bounces with every step. There's something so cheerful about her. Her dad calls her Sunshine, and it's a nickname that I use occasionally, too. She's sweet, happy, and light and always has been.

I look down at my pants. I've tucked my erection in my waistband, but it's throbbing angrily. It knows what it wants, even though it'll never get it. Her dad would blow my balls off with his shotgun, and that'd only be the first step.

"Down, boy."

But my erection persists, and I have to resort to something that has happened with increasing frequency this summer.

I go to the private bathroom connected to my office, unzip my pants, pull out my dick, and close my eyes.

* * *

Camilla is kneeling in front of me, her big brown eyes wide. Her full lips are pouting, ready for my cock, but I'm not ready to give it to her.

Not until she begs.

"Please, sir."

I close my eyes, her sweet voice so seductive that it's hard not to give it to her.

"Convince me that you want it."

"I need it," she murmurs, her eyes heating up. "I need to suck your cock."

I rub the tip against her cheek. She turns her head, trying to take it into her mouth, but I pull away before she can.

"How much do you need it?"

"More than anything in the world." She licks her lips. "I need it more than anything ever."

My hand caresses her jaw, and then I'm forcing her mouth open as I shove the entire length inside. She gasps and gags a little as I enter her throat. Her hands are bound behind her back with handcuffs, so she has no control in this situation. There are tears in her eyes from the suddenness of my entry.

My hands slide into her hair. She's obediently sucking me into her mouth. I watch each time as I thrust and retreat, thrust and retreat. My balls draw up and I feel the tingle in my spine that means that I'm ready to shoot.

One of my hands slides to the back of her neck, holding her right where I want her as I grunt and unload my seed into her wet, warm mouth.

"Swallow," I tell her. "Take it all."

I watch her throat work as she tries to swallow all of it, but it's too much for her. A little white come is coming out of the corner of her mouth.

* * *

I open my eyes, panting a little from the force of my orgasm. I clean up and flush everything down the toilet.

She makes me hard several times a day. If I ignore it, my blue balls make it clear that I need to unload in her. I've barely been able to control myself, and only the thought of castration and betraying my friend Jack stop me from acting on my fantasies. But I know that it would ruin everything.

One more week, and I'll have my normal secretary Amanda back. One more week, and temptation will go back to school full-time. I'm about to

go insane.

This week can't end soon enough.

Email

Lincoln

The next afternoon, I'm coming in from a lunch meeting when I see her. She has big headphones on. They're connected to her phone while she sorts through all the email that has accumulated in the last day.

"Camilla."

She flushes the same way as she pushes her headphones off so that they're around her neck.

"How can I help you, sir?"

"I need you to get me a double shot of espresso from the café next door as soon as possible." I need the caffeine. I'd like to be drinking some whiskey, but it's a little early in the day for that. Plus alcohol lowering my inhibitions is a terrible idea when all I want to do is bend my best friend's daughter over my desk and fuck her until she's screaming my name so that the whole office can hear her and know that she's mine.

Bad idea.

"Sure, sir."

"And you can grab something for yourself. Put it on the company account."

"Right away." She stands up, tugging her skirt down. Her breasts jiggle just a little bit. God, everything she does entrances me. She makes me think like a horny teenager. I'm surprised that there isn't drool dripping off my chin.

She has it all: beauty, brains, efficiency, and a sense of humor. If she were two decades older, we'd be married already.

She walks towards the elevator. I'm admiring her smooth, sexy walk before I shake my head and turn around. I'm about to head into my office when I see the email that's on her screen.

The subject line says "Today's Lincoln Fantasy".

I know that I'm snooping into a private file, but come on. My name is there. Surely that gives me a free pass.

I look around the office. Nobody is paying attention. The sales team that is normally on this floor is out at some corporate retreat, setting sales goals for the next quarter. The people who are here aren't looking at me.

I sit down at her desk and read the rest of it.

* * *

Oh my god, Kelly, I can't stop thinking about him. I want his perfect mouth on mine. I want him to pin me against the wall and hold me in place until I beg him to stop because I can't take any more. And then I want him to keep going anyway.

I can't handle working here anymore, Kels. It's going to be hell this week. It's only Tuesday, so I have three more days to go.

I'm so wet that I think that I've soaked through my panties and onto my skirt. Just smelling his scent makes me wet. He doesn't even have to be here.

I can never tell him that I want him to shove me face-down on his desk, tie my hands with his tie, and *fuck me until my mind explodes into a*

thousand pieces. He'll tell my dad that

I was inappropriate at work, and then

I'll get yelled at. I don't want to be cut

off.

* * *

My eyebrows are raised. She was

afraid of me telling her dad how she

felt? Not a chance in hell, not if I

wanted to keep my balls. He'd show up

at my office with a shotgun in a

heartbeat.

She felt the same way. My mind

ran through the possibilities.

She shouldn't worry about being cut off. I can provide for her as easily as her father can. Better, even, since I'd never make her work just for the sake of working.

Maybe I should plan a surprise for when she comes back with my coffee.

Coffee

Camilla

The coffee is almost too hot to handle. I know that the cup's material is supposed to insulate it, but it's almost hot enough to scorch my hand. I was in such a hurry to get back that I forgot to get coffee collars. I don't want to go back and get some. I hope Lincoln doesn't yell at me for forgetting.

No, that's dumb. He doesn't yell at me for stupid stuff. He's demanding and expects perfection, but he'd never yell at me for forgetting a coffee collar for his cup. He's pretty fair.

He comes down like the wrath of God when he's provoked, though. One of the financial analysts forgot to send him a sales report before a meeting once, and I listened when he ripped the analyst a new one.

I'd been so turned on that after I listened to the fury in his voice, I'd gone to the bathroom and taken care of myself. He never let people forget who was in charge.

I am quickly forgetting how hot the coffee I'm holding is. I hit the elevator button for the top floor with my elbow. Three more days of working as his assistant, and then all of this will be over.

It'll be a relief, but I'm also afraid that I'll regret not making a move on him when I had the chance. He probably sees me as nothing more than a little girl, but I've had a crush on him forever. My dad snores, but he doesn't.

I know, since I've slept so close to him in the mountains time and time again.

My hands tighten a little on the coffee cups, but then the heat makes me loosen my grip.

Three more days.

When I get back to our corner of the office, I see that his door is open. I walk into his office and see him staring at his computer screen.

"I brought your coffee, sir." I never called him sir before I came to work for him, but it seems respectful. Polite. It creates a good employee-boss relationship.

"Camilla, stay in here for a moment, please." It's not a question. I put both coffee cups down on his desk.

"The grande one is for you." I only have a decaf tall latte, because it's afternoon and I'll be up until midnight if I drink caffeinated anything right now.

"Could you close the door?"

My heart jumps at a request so close to yesterday's fantasy, but I'm being dumb. He's just asking me to close a door, not to get naked and sweaty with him. I curse my brain for giving me a full-color visual of what that would be like, my soft body beneath his hard one. We've gone swimming in lakes. I know that he has tight, hard muscles and washboard abs. He definitely doesn't look like your average pencil pusher.

"Sure thing."

I stand up and close the door. I hear the small thud.

"And lock it."

My heart starts beating so fast and hard that I can hear it in my ears.

"Lock it?" I turn to him with a little panic in my eyes. I have no idea what's going on.

"Lock it," he repeats. I know that he's waiting for me to do it. With an audible gulp, I turn the lock.

Reading

Lincoln

When she spins around, her nipples are hard, poking out.

"Come over here." The coffee cups are sitting on one corner of my desk. She sits down in the chair in front of my desk.

"What do you need, sir?" She looks like I'm going to pull out an iron maiden or something.

"I want to talk to you about your emails."

"What emails?" I can see her pulse pick up in her throat.

"The ones that you've been sending to your best friend, Kelly."

Her face gets a little paler. "I can't...you haven't...did you read them?"

"I did."

If possible, she grows even more pale.

"I can explain."

I motion for her to continue. Her hand goes to twirl a curl around her finger.

"I just...I can't..."

I stand up and put a finger on her lips.

"I read all of them."

Instead of going pale, her face flushes. I smile slowly, even though I know she's deeply embarrassed. I sit back in my chair.

"Are you going to tell my dad?" she squeaks. "Please, please don't."

"Hush, sweetheart. That's not what I had in mind."

"Then why am I here?" She turns to look at the locked door. "And why is the door locked?"

"Do you know how stringent the sexual harassment policies are here?"

"No." She turns back to look at me.

"They're very strict. I made them myself. My mother was sexually harassed by her boss for decades, and I swore that it would never happen in any company that I was the head of. Not on my watch."

She nods. "Protecting women. I get it."

"And that's the reason why we can't act on your little fantasies. Like the one where I pin you against the wall and make you come even when you tell me to stop."

"You read that?!" she squeaks. "I haven't even sent that one yet."

"I read them all, the ones you sent and the ones that are drafts. They're all on your corporate email, so you have no reasonable expectation of privacy.

You're very imaginative, Camilla." My tongue caresses her name.

"What's going to happen now?"

"I thought you'd never ask." I stood up. "I want you to take off your skirt."

"But I...but you just said...sexual harassment policies..."

"Now, Camilla."

She stands up and reaches behind her to unzip her skirt. The position is pushing her breasts out, and they didn't need it. Her young breasts are firm, full, and perky, the sort of thing that you find in a centerfold. Her buttons are straining to contain her breasts, and I can see some hints of smooth, golden brown skin.

She's wearing a tiny black lace thong that barely covers anything. She's standing there, her face flushed, uncertain of what's going to happen next. Her skirt is on the ground.

"I can't touch you, Camilla. I can't do it while you're on the payroll."

"Then why is my skirt off?" She blinks at me, a hint of fear in her brown eyes.

"Because you're going to touch yourself, Camilla."

She gasps a little, her eyes getting big. "But I...I've never..."

"You've never masturbated in front of anyone else before?"

She nods.

"How old are you?"

"Nineteen," she whispers.

Nineteen. So young. I have no business doing this with a girl that young.

But there's a devil inside me that says, "Put your hand in the front of your panties."

I watch as her hand settles on the front of the sweet junction of her thighs.

"Now rub your clit until you come."

"Standing?"

I motion to the couch in my office.

"Laying down. Spread your legs."

She walks over to the couch, her hand still trapped in her thong, and she lays down. Her legs are far apart now, and I bless her regular yoga practice.

"Like this?"

The thong is annoying me, obstructing my view of her pussy.

"Take your thong off."

She takes her hand out and pulls off her thong.

"And your shirt."

She unbuttons each button slowly. Her hands are shaking. Arousal, excitement, and a hint of fear, I think. Anybody could come up to my door and find it locked. It wouldn't take a genius to realize that Camilla was inside my office with me.

Her generous breasts are filling up a black lace push-up bra. God, I want to take those luscious mounds into my mouth. I clench my fists.

Three more days. Then I can have her every way that I want.

"Pleasure yourself," I order. "I want to see you come on my couch while I read one of your emails to you."

Her eyes meet mine as her hand goes between her legs again. Soon, she's rubbing herself back and forth, back and forth. I have to unzip myself before my pants strangle my erection. I'm slowly stroking myself to the sight of her spread out on my couch.

The smell of her arousal fills the air. I can feel myself release a little pre-come.

* * *

I can't believe the suit he was wearing today. He's always hot, Kels, but today he was a god.

I think that a woman must have hand-made that suit for him, because it loves him. Everything that he wears fits well, but this suit looks even better than the others.

His red power tie is giving me ideas. I want him to call me into his office and then shove me down on his couch, forcing my legs apart and tying my hands above my head. I want him to dry hump me until we're both ready. Then he'll tear my skirt and thong off before going down on me. Once I've come, he'll ride me until neither of us can move.

* * *

I can hear her moan a little.

"Keep going," I encourage her.

I don't think that she needs encouragement. Her eyes are closed. She's panting fast now. I can see her breasts move with each quick intake of breath.

"Mmm," she moans quietly. Her legs are shaking. Her mouth is open. Her back is arching as she shakes all over from her orgasm in front of me.

Then it's over. My cock is still hard, but I tuck it back into my pants. This time is for her, not for me.

"Beautiful," I say, and she opens her eyes to stare right at me. She looks at her juice-covered hand likc it belongs to a stranger and blushes hard.

"I don't know...what just happened."

"Do you want me to recap for you? In detail?"

She's sitting up on my couch now. "No!" She goes to get the skirt from where she dropped it earlier. I enjoy the sight of her bent over, her ass perfectly displayed for me. She pulls it up around her hips. She searches for her thong, but I say, "Leave it."

"Leave what?"

"Your thong. I want to smell it while I wait for you."

She's speechless, her mouth opening and closing without a word coming out.

"We're done here," I say, before she can recover. "And you can go home now. I'll see you tomorrow."

She never took off her shoes. I hear them click as she goes to the door, unlocks it, and heads back to her desk.

I don't know if the other people out there will smell her arousal on her. I'm torn whether I want them to or not. On one hand, I'm skating close to the edge of a sexual harassment lawsuit. On the other, I want them to know that I've been pleasuring her.

I look at the two cups of coffee on my desk. I drink the grande one, even though it's gone a little cold. I drink a sip of hers, too, so that I'll know her drink order.

It tastes foul. Decaf. I dump it out in my sink. Well, if that's what she

wants, that's what she'll get. Whatever
she wants.

Last Day

Camilla

THREE DAYS LATER

It's Friday, my last day of work.

I'm about to go back to school now.

Lincoln has been nothing but professional after that time in his office. I almost think that I imagined it. I haven't even told Kelly about it, and she's already asked me why I stopped sending her my fantasies via email when we're both at work. I don't want to tell her about it. It seems like a secret, perfect dream. Even if the whole thing was a figment of my imagination, I'm going to hold it in my heart until the end of time.

The look in his eyes when he watched me. The warmth of his voice when he read my email to me. The sound of his hand going up and down his hard cock. All those things were incredible.

My phone buzzes, telling me that the alarm that I set for five o'clock is on. Half the people in the office telecommute on Fridays, and the other half are out early. It's the weekend now. Lincoln and I are the only ones still in the office.

Lincoln is in his office, so I knock on the door.

"Link?" I open the door and walk into his office. I can see big stacks of paper on his desk. He's overseeing some acquisition of a tech company that has an app that we'd like to have.

"Yeah?"

"I'm out. Thanks for giving me a job. I'll see you when you come over for dinner."

"Come here and close the door."

He looks like a lion who hasn't been fed in months. I kind of feel like running away, but my traitorous nipples are getting hard, remembering what it was like to stretch out on his couch.

"I don't know if that's a good idea."

"You don't work for me anymore. I think that it's a great idea. But it's your choice."

I look at the open door and then at Lincoln.

And then I close it.

His smile is bright.

"That's what I hoped you'd choose." He's untying his tie now.

"I wore the red one today. I know you like it."

I can feel my breathing pick up a little.

"Are you going to..."

"Play out one of your fantasies? You bet."

He comes towards me and crowds me against the wall.

"Hands up above your head."

Staring into his eyes, I can see the blackness expand as I put my hands above my head. Then he's briskly tying them together.

Then his hard body is pushing me against the wall. I can feel myself getting wet. His hard erection is digging into my stomach.

"Is this as good as you imagined?"

I shiver. "Better."

I'm wearing pants today. His hands are on my pant's button, and then he's unzipping them and pulling my pants and thong down around my ankles. He pulls off one shoe carefully, and then he's pulling off the other. My pants and thong are on the ground.

"Kneel."

I kneel in front of him. I've never sucked anybody off before, but I'm glad that it's him.

My hands might be tied together, but I can still use them. I've learned enough from Kelly to know that I need to put a fist around whatever I can't fit inside of my mouth.

I lean it but he backs away.

"You have to want it."

I lean forward, grab his cock, tug it, and then put it into my mouth. I hum a little around it, which makes him gasp. I can feel him shoot a little pre-come into my mouth, which I swallow.

Then I'm stroking his cock, using the smooth silk of his tie, and fondling his balls as he thrusts back and forth inside of my mouth.

"Uh. Ah."

A salty stream of seed is spilling inside of my mouth. I swallow it up, maintaining eye contact with him as he unloads inside of my mouth.

Then it's over. He pulls his cock out of my mouth. I know that it's softening, but my mouth feels so empty now.

"You're going to bend over my desk now."

I look at his desk, still covered in stacks of paper.

"But what about the acquisition?"

He shoves everything off of his desk. The papers spill onto the floor, covering the carpet with papers that are rapidly getting mixed with each other. They're out of order.

"I don't give a fuck about the acquisition. You. Desk. Now. Or you're going to get a spanking that you won't forget."

I rush to his desk and bend over.

"Good girl," he praises. I'm still wearing a shirt and bra. His desk is cold against my cheek. I'm breathing, waiting for him to touch me.

Then a hand is between my thighs. I jump when he finally touches me there, right there.

"Responsive little thing, aren't you?"

A thick finger pushes its way inside of me. Then he stops.

"You're a virgin."

I'm as wet as a fountain.

"Yes." My whisper is very quiet in this office.

His finger pulls out of me. "Oh God, this is a mistake."

I cringe when I hear him call finger-fucking me a mistake. I can feel tears threaten, so I go to the corner where my clothes are. I put on my skirt, not bothering with my thong. Another few seconds and my shoes are on.

"Camilla. Look at me." I stare at the ground and try not to let the tears fall.

Then his hand is on my chin and he's forcing me to look up at him.

I can't stop the tears from falling anymore.

"Camilla, baby." He holds me close and rests his chin on the top of my head. "Your first time belongs to someone you love, not your dirty boss. Not your dad's best friend, who, by the way, will slaughter me if he ever hears that I touched his baby daughter."

I stiffen in his arms and pull away. "I'm not a little girl anymore."

He puts a finger in his mouth, keeping eye contact with me. He sucks it then pulls it out with a pop.

"I know." He sighs. "But I can't take your virginity."

Tears of rage and sexual frustration are running down my cheeks now.

"Well, it's moot," I say, not bothering to wipe them away. "Because it's my last day of work anyway."

Barbarian

Lincoln

I watch Camilla walk out, thong in her hand, a sad slowness to her walk, and I feel like a total piece of shit. I never should have touched her, and I definitely shouldn't have gotten within a whisper of taking her virginity. For God's sake, I remember the day she was born. I remember her selling me Samoas when she was a Brownie. I remember how proud her father was when she graduated from high school.

I'd betrayed him. Smelling her scent on my hand, though, maybe made it worth it. I lick up the rest of it.

I felt her melting on me like warm honey. I knew she wanted it. And I'd still sent her away.

I must be a fool. An honorable one.

I wash my hands, then I'm pulling out my phone. So many contacts. There's a blonde who doesn't expect anything besides a dinner and a good time. A brunette who loves to argue with me and then hate fuck me because she says that I'm a corporate pig who needs to be taught a lesson. She normally "teaches" by ripping my clothes. A red-head who loves tossing salad.

And all of them pale in comparison to what I just had with Camilla, and we haven't even fucked yet.

I'm a mess.

I'm still hard. My dick is about to poke a hole in my pants, so I shuffle into my bathroom and close the door.

In my imagination, she hasn't left.

* * *

There she is, bent over on my desk. My finger touches her hymen. I don't say anything, just silently thank God that she's giving me this precious gift.

I kneel behind her, pulling her thighs apart until I can lick up all her honey. She shivers in front of me as I bury my face inside of her, but just not deep enough. The angle against the desk is pushing her clit against the hard edge, and she's moaning in front of me. Her legs are shaking because she's about to come.

I thrust two fingers inside of her small opening and she's shouting as I press against that perfect spot on the front wall that makes her go wild. Her come is on my hand, filling the air with the scent of sex.

She's shaking on my desk when I stand up, my cock ready to go even after she sucked me off.

I tease her entrance with the tip. She pushes her hips back, but I step back.

"I control the pace here," I warn. "Not you. Against the desk."

She settles down against the desk. To punish her, I don't penetrate her with my cock. Instead, a finger gathers some of the moisture that's spreading to her thighs and circles around her back door.

"Do you want me to take your anal virginity, too?"

"Yes." The whisper is almost too quiet to hear. God, she's so dirty. A dirty virgin. I love it.

"I'll have to prepare you first, make sure that I don't hurt you."

"I trust you." Her body is on my desk. Her hands are tied. She has no power in this position.

I sink my cock into her slowly, one inch at a time. I can feel her muscles already fluttering around me.

"You like this?"

Her cry means that she's beyond words, but the quick clenching of her muscles around my dick say that she'll come soon.

"Come," I command. "Now."

With a scream, she's clenching my cock tighter than a fist. I can't shoot when she's this tight. I can see that her leg muscles are clenched up. She arches up and I pull her hair so that her back curves like a C.

She's panting hard beneath me. I put a hand on her throat, not to choke her, though. I'm just feel her pulse and each breath as she finishes her orgasm.

Then my hand slides to the base of her neck and I'm controlling her motion as I slam my cock into her small body. She's still gasping in front of me, but I'm a barbarian. I'm not polite, not gentle. I'm invading her, claiming her as my own.

I'm not wearing a condom. The realization sparks my orgasm as I fill her with my seed. I imagine what her small body would look like with a baby bump, what she would look like with my baby inside of her.

I am pouring jet after jet of seed into her body, too much for it to hold. It's already leaking out onto her thighs.

* * *

I clean myself up again. Damn.

Sending her away like a gentleman

might have been the right thing to do,

but I couldn't have a date with anyone

but my hand. When I think about other

women, my dick shrivels up. It is

Camilla or no one at all.

Strawberry Bubble Bath

Camilla

When I get home, my dad isn't there. My mom died when she had me, so it is just the two of us and a part-time housekeeper who thankfully isn't working today.

I run to my room and go to my bathtub. I need to wash away his hands on my skin.

I fill up my tub and dump in some strawberry bubble bath. Then I step in.

The smell is already making me happier.

I start to wash myself off, rubbing his scent off of me, but touching my slick skin reminds me of him. My eyes close as I think up yet another fantasy.

* * *

"Show me your tits," he growls.

I quickly take off my shirt and bra, dumping them on the floor next to the couch. I'm sprawled out, legs wide, just like he likes. My thong is in his hand. He's sniffing it.

Then he's on his feet, coming over to straddle my body on his couch. It's a tight fit, but he's managing it. His cock is out of his pants, but he's still mostly clothed.

He has pre-come dripping out of it, and his hand is spreading it all over himself before he puts his dick in the center of my chest.

"Push your tits together."

My hands are on the outside of my breasts, pushing them together, creating a soft tunnel.

His eyes are closed as he starts to pump his dick through my breasts. His mouth is hanging open. His dick comes very close to my mouth every time he thrusts forward. He's thrusting in a steady rhythm. I'm watching his dick come close to my mouth every other second.

So I stick out my tongue and lick him on an upstroke.

He roars as he shoots his come on my face, on my tits, on my neck, everywhere.

When he's done, he kisses me gently.

"You're so perfect for me, Camilla. I love you."

* * *

I'm crying now. The bath water is getting cold. I smell like strawberries and regret. I'm sad that I want someone who won't take my virginity. I don't think I mean much to him. Kelly lost hers to a boyfriend when she was sixteen, but I've held onto mine. It's always been a fantasy of mine that I'd lose it to Lincoln.

Stupid girl.

He doesn't care about me. He wants me to find someone who loves me, which means that he definitely doesn't. The only time he'll ever tell me that he loves me is in my daydreams.

My tears are dripping down my cheeks and into the bath water. I pull the plug out of the drain and watch the suds slide down the drain, just like all my hopes and dreams.

Camping

Camilla

ONE YEAR AGO

"I'm going to scout that unmarked trail that the volunteers told us about. I'll be back in three hours. You two make dinner, okay?" My dad likes alone time, so it's not a surprise that he's disappearing for a little while. He likes to leave me by myself for a while on the weekends.

But this time, I'm not alone.

"Sure," Lincoln tells him cheerfully. "We'll make dinner before you get back."

"Are you sure it's safe? I mean, they just cut it. Not a lot of people have used it lately."

"It's fine," my dad says. "Just grill some trout and I'll be back before you know it. We still have some sweet potatoes left. I'll be back before dark."

He walks into the forest. I can see his backpack get smaller and smaller as he goes deeper into the forest, and then he turns and the trees hide him. I can still hear him walking, but the sound is fading.

And now I'm alone with his best friend, also known as my lifelong crush. When I was five, I told everyone at my birthday party that my birthday wish was to marry Lincoln, which made everyone there hysterical. Except for his mean fiancée, Marcia. She gave me the stink eye and spent the rest of my birthday party drinking a lot of wine. She only lasted for a week after that, though.

Link hadn't ever said much about it, other than that she was totally psycho.

"I'll grill the trout if you take care of the sweet potatoes."

"Deal."

I bend over to hunt through our supplies. It takes me a minute to finally find the bag of sweet potatoes, which is a lot smaller than I thought it would be. There's a roll of aluminum foil next to it. When I turn around with the bag of sweet potatoes and foil in my hands, I can see Lincoln staring at me.

"Are you okay?"

"Yeah." He swallows. "I need to get the salt and pepper from our supplies."

He kneels down to grab the seasoning for the fish. It's simple, but my dad told me that he prefers freshly caught mountain trout to any meal from a fancy restaurant.

That's why we're out here. It's supposed to be my eighteenth birthday celebration, but really it's an excuse for my dad to run away from his life as a corporate big shot and go fishing in the woods. He's constantly surrounded by people at work, so he loves to hear the sounds of nature when nobody's near him.

We work in silence for a moment, side by side next to the small campfire. I'm wrapping the sweet potatoes completely in foil so I can put them at the edges of the campfire. Technically, the sweet potatoes are supposed to cook in the ashes, but my dad has never been patient enough to wait to do them separately.

"I think that it's okay now."

Lincoln stands up. The fish are on a spit, roasting above the fire. The smell of cooking fish and burning wood fills the little clearing where we have our tents.

"Now we wait." The campfire isn't that big or that hot, so it'll slowly cook everything. I tuck a strand of hair behind my ear.

"What do you want to do while we wait? Play cards?" Lincoln looks at me like I'm the little girl he taught to play Go Fish.

"I'm going to take a nap." I smile at him and go into my tent. I open my jeans. I can't make a sound, but being so close to my crush is killing me. I don't really date. No high school boy could ever compare to Lincoln.

His scent mingled with the smell of our campfire turned me on. To be honest, his scent would turn me on without the fire.

I put my hand on my most sensitive spot and closed my eyes.

* * *

"On your hands and knees."

I hesitate.

"I'm not going to ask you twice."

His voice is soft, but the tone doesn't leave room for resistance.

I bend over the log that we pulled next to the campfire. I can feel the hard wood under my soft stomach. My hands are in the dirt.

I can feel his hands under me, unbuttoning my pants, unzipping them, and pulling them and my underwear down. The wind touches me between my thighs, a gentle caress that makes me a little cold. I shiver.

His huge hand settles on one soft ass cheek.

"I've been watching this ass swing while we've been hiking all day." Without warning, his hand comes down to strike me.

I cry out, startled and in a little pain. The pain mingles with pleasure as he softly strokes me where he just hit me.

"You like that." A finger is testing me, pushing inside of me. I'm soaking wet.

Then he's sliding my wetness up to travel to my back door.

"Oh! Please don't!" I yelp. "Don't touch me there."

"I'm not going to hurt you," he says, his voice like black magic. "Relax, baby."

"Okay."

I take a deep breath and relax as his finger explores my back hole. Then he's pushing the tip of one finger inside of me. I don't know if I like it. I moan as he stimulates places inside of me that I didn't even know existed.

A climax hits me like a semi-truck going 20 over the speed limit. No warning, but my body is soaring from the impact.

* * *

I open my eyes and hope I didn't make too much noise while I touched myself. I hunt for my makeup remover wipes to clean off my hand, which smells like me now. I ball up the wipe and shove it into my trash bag. I hope my dad never knows what I did. If he ever knew that I fantasized about his best friend putting a finger up my ass, he'd probably check me into an insane

asylum or something.

Cold Water

Lincoln

Camilla is in her tent taking a nap while her dad is out, which means that I have a rare moment to myself. I take a look at the food that's cooking. If it turns into a raging bonfire, Camilla will notice. Or she'll be asleep and all of our gear will go up in smoke.

It's pretty small, though, and we sheltered it from the wind. I don't waver when I pour some water on it.

The fish is done anyway, and the sweet potatoes will be fine in the ashes.

I had gotten hard watching Camilla bend over, and my erection hadn't gone away. I'm lucky that her dad didn't come back, because he probably would've slaughtered me and left my body for the bears if he understood how I felt about his daughter. A daughter who was growing more beautiful and womanly by the day. If I didn't want to spontaneously combust, I'd need to take care of some things.

There is a mountain stream just two minutes from camp. If Camilla needs me, I am within screaming distance.

When I'm right next to the stream, I strip. It isn't deep, but it is cold. Ice melt is never that nice. I try to pour ice water over my dick, but it refuses to go down. Looks like I have a date with my hand.

* * *

It's past midnight, and my buddy is sleeping off all the Jack that we drank. I'm wide awake, and the alcohol has wiped away my scruples. He's snoring away in our tent, so I unzip the opening and go out to Camilla's tent. I unzip it as quietly as I can. I can see just a little slow, steady movement in the scanty moonlight that tells me that she's breathing deeply, sleeping like an angel.

I lay down on top of her sleeping bag. I put a hand over her mouth and lean in. I whisper in her ear. "Camilla, wake up."

Her eyes are barely open. She's saying something muffled by my hand.

"Camilla, you have to be quiet." I thrust my erection at her. Even through the sleeping bag, she can feel it. She stills.

"Camilla, I'm going to let go. If you don't want this, tell me now. Otherwise, stay quiet."

I take my hand away. All I can hear is the hooting of an owl. Her breaths are coming faster and faster.

I have my answer. I pull apart her sleeping bag, yanking down her pajama pants and underwear. I pull her legs over my shoulders so I can pile drive her. If we had privacy, I'd take my time. Her father, my best friend, is sleeping only feet away. Tent walls aren't much of a barrier.

One hand goes between her legs. She's wet enough for me to take right now, but I rub her for a few minutes anyway. I can tell from her heavy breathing that she's trying very hard not to make any noise. Neither of us wants to get busted.

I stop rubbing her and guide my dick inside of her tight pussy. She's incredibly warm on a cool night like this. I feel like I'm sinking into a sauna.

I hear her panting very quietly. I thrust all the way, and I hear a muffled gasp. Then I can't hold myself back any longer and begin to swing my hips as quietly as I can, getting as deep as I can. Her muscles are contracting around me, fluttering, as I hold back my own groan of completion. She's filled with my come. I want her to keep it, but I know that there'd be hell to pay if she smelled like me tomorrow morning.

I fumble in the corner for those wet wipes that she brought with her, the ones that we've been using to wipe our hands before eating. I clean her between her thighs before wiping myself off. I throw the wipe into the garbage bag she keeps in her tent.

"Don't tell anyone." She's still half-naked under me and my dick wants her again, but we've taken enough risks for tonight.

I disengage her legs from my shoulders, then I lean down to kiss her, slow and soft. She kisses me back timidly at first, then she pushes her tongue inside of my mouth.

And she's not an innocent little girl anymore. Yeah, she's eighteen, but she's a woman.

* * *

When I open my eyes, I'm standing in a cold mountain stream that's carried away my come. I shake myself off and put on my clothes, even though I'm still a little wet. I walk back to camp.

It's so damned inconvenient to want my best friend's little girl. Maybe it's just the prolonged exposure, having to be in close quarters all the time. I wonder if any of the women in my little black book would mind being called Camilla while we fuck.

Dress Hunt

Camilla

NOW

I rinse off, then I find my ratty pajamas. They're really old but the most comfortable clothing that I own. They're pink, but sort of a grayish pink after all this time. I should've thrown them away years ago, but they make me feel safe.

I tuck myself into bed with my Kindle, arranging my pillows so I'm in a cozy nest. Then I hear the garage door open. My dad is home.

"Where are you, Sunshine?"

I get out of bed and go to the mezzanine. "Here, Dad."

"Have you eaten yet?"

"No. I'm not very hungry."

"I thought that we'd celebrate your last day of working. It'll be good for us to spend time together before you have to go back to school. I made a reservation for seven at your favorite place, that Italian restaurant. I invited Lincoln."

Oh, shit.

He sees my face. "Something wrong, Sunshine?"

"Nope." I shake my head. "I'll just get changed and we can head out."

I go into my room and throw open my closet. What's appropriate for a celebratory dinner with my father and his best friend, the one who almost fucked me today but stopped because I am a virgin?

I hate everything in my closet. The periwinkle blue dress makes me look like I'm 12. I have a royal blue dress with pretty embroidery, but the neckline is too high. It's hard, because I need a neckline low enough to tantalize Lincoln but high enough to pass my dad's scrutiny.

I have a black dress with white stripes that I discard because they make me look wide. There's a dress covered in flowers that makes me look like a little girl.

I don't have anything to wear. I growl at my closet and wonder how angry my dad would be if I insisted on going to the mall to buy a new dress for tonight when our reservation is so soon.

I dig deeper into my closet. Then I see it.

The perfect dress is sitting there. I bought it on a dare from Kelly. She said that my clothes were too boring.

It sort of reminds me of a flamenco dancer's costume, but there is a daring slit up the side that reveals a little leg when I walked. Tantalizing without actually showing anything.

I choose high-heeled ankle boots under the dress. I need three-inch heels because the skirt is so long.

I put on a very small amount of makeup. My dad knows that I didn't wear much, so it would look weird if I showed up looking like a circus clown. I just put a little eyeliner on to emphasize my eyes, which everyone always tells me are beautiful. I look at my single tube of red lipstick but leave it alone. It'd be gone in a half minute when we started eating even if I did put it on.

I go downstairs in my ankle boots and pretty dress that looked demure until I walked. My dad is staring at his phone.

"Ready, Sunshine?"

"Ready, Dad."

We walk into the garage. I slide into the passenger seat of his Lexus. Then we're roaring out into the city.

Under the Table

Lincoln

I'm sitting at our table already when they arrive. He's wearing the suit he probably wore to work today. She's wearing a stunning dress.

Everything's covered, but when she walks, I can see a flash of leg. I find her legs very arousing. Fuck, I find every bit of her arousing.

"Hope you haven't been waiting long."

"Nah," I say, taking a sip of my wine. I need it to get through this dinner. It'd be too weird for me to turn it down, especially since he knows that I'm not seeing anyone right now.

They sit down across the table from me. Camilla is directly in front of me. A waiter bustles over.

"What can I get for you, sir? Miss?"

"A glass of your house red for me and some orange juice for her."

"Right away, sir."

"So how was your day? Busy? You're getting your secretary Amanda back, so that's good."

"Yeah." I take another sip of wine. "It's good."

I don't know why, but the restaurant's lighting is making Camilla's face even more beautiful than usual. It is highlighting her smooth cheekbones and full lips. She looks like an ancient queen of a civilization long gone. She might be a teenager, but she looks like a woman.

"Are you glad to be going back to school, Camilla?" I ask politely. It would be weird if we didn't speak at this dinner for the three of us.

"I'm very glad." She smiles with just her mouth. Her eyes are angry and cold, but I don't think that her dad has noticed. "Can't wait to get back into the swing of college life."

"Those were the days, huh?" My buddy nudges me. "Wild girls, crazy parties, staying out past dawn. Can't keep up with all that anymore. You're not drinking of course, Sunshine, right?"

"I wouldn't tell you if I did drink, Dad." She rolls her eyes at him, but he just laughs.

"You should keep some secrets from your old man. Just don't turn up unmarried and pregnant on my doorstep one day and I'll believe that I raised you right."

Her face is getting a little pink. "I don't..."

"I know you're a good kid, Sunshine. I'm just teasing you." He turns to me. "I was blessed with an incredible kid. Too bad you don't have one of your own, you know. I thought that you'd be married by now, but you've enjoyed the bachelor life. You can sow your wild oats wherever you like."

At the mention of wild oats, I feel a gentle brush against my cock. I think that I'm imagining it until I see Camilla's eyes. They're fiery and angry.

The touch comes again, firmer this time. The little minx is sliding her foot up and down my dick. She's trying to get me back for turning her down. My cock does not care. It's rock hard and ready to go. I can already feel a little pre-come oozing out of the tip.

I try to warn her to stop with my eyes, but she's ignoring it.

I grunt.

"You okay, Link?"

"That was my stomach," I lie. "I'm hungry."

"Food will be here soon enough. What do you think about the weather lately?" He launches into a monologue that I can't keep track of because I'm breaking out in a sweat. I'm about to come under this table from her little foot rubbing up against me. I can't move because it'll look weird. I can't run to the bathroom, because then everyone will see my erection proudly displayed. I grit my teeth and close my eyes as I feel myself release in my pants like a teenage boy.

I open my eyes to see victory shining in her eyes. I know that she's mad, but I didn't expect her revenge to be a foot job during dinner with her father. She's diabolical. I need to clean up. My cock is softening now.

"Excuse me," I mutter, and her father doesn't stop for a second. "I'm going to hit the bathroom."

Following

Camilla

I just did something bad, and I'm planning on following it up with something worse.

My dad must have had a glass or three while I was changing, because he's cheerfully talking to two ladies who are sitting at the table next to ours. His voice is a little loud.

"I'm going to the bathroom."

My dad doesn't skip a beat, just goes right on talking about the weather and climate change. I don't know if he even needs an audience.

I go to the back hallway where the restrooms are. I pass some guy who is still zipping up his pants. The door to the guys' restroom is closing very slowly. There's only one stall and nobody at the urinals. If Link is in there, he's in the stall. I hope no guys need to use the restroom for the next ten minutes, because I go inside, shove the door shut despite some resistance, and lock it.

"Link," I whisper.

"Camilla." The door of the stall swings open. He sticks his head out. "Get out of the men's bathroom."

Instead of obeying, I push the stall door open. He has his erection in his hand. He was hiding it behind the door.

"Are you close?" I can see a little pearly liquid at the tip.

I kneel on the tile floor, ignoring the fact that my dress is definitely getting dirty.

"Camilla, you can't be in here."

When I pull his dick into my mouth, though, he shuts up.

"Mmm." He tastes nice. I suck him like I haven't eaten all day.

"Camilla, we're going to get caught."

I don't dignify that with a response. I'm playing with his balls now, sucking him deep into my mouth.

Then he's spurting seed straight into my mouth. I drain him dry, sucking even when I think everything is gone.

"Jesus Christ, Camilla."

I stand up, wiping my mouth with the back of my hand.

"Don't send me away again," I warn him. "You won't like the consequences."

Suddenly, my feet are no longer on the ground. He has me pinned up against the wall, my legs around his waist.

"Don't threaten me, Camilla." The small thread of menace in his voice turns me on.

He has me pushed up against the wall, his hand going to the slit in my full skirt and going straight for my honeypot. His fingers go directly in.

"I knew it. I knew you were already wet for me."

All I can say is a small wordless moan as he circles my clit with some of my wetness.

"You're ready to go off like a little rocket, aren't you?"

He does something with his fingers that makes my eyes roll back in my head. When I can think again, he slowly lowers me until I'm on my feet again.

"I'm going to give you what you've been asking for." His hand settles on the top curve of my ass. "And you're going to like it."

"What about my dad?"

"We'll figure it out." A muscle ticks in his jaw. "He's going to hear about it sometime."

We both wash our hands in the sink. Someone is banging on the door.

"Hey! I have to use the toilet."

Link unlocks the door and shields me from the guy outside, who is trying to get a good look at me.

Mistaken

Camilla

Link and I make our way back to the table. It's totally normal for us to go to the bathroom at the same time.

"What, did you two guzzle a few gallons of water at work at the same time?" My dad's face shows that he's pretty drunk. The ladies at the table next to us are giggling.

"Something like that," Link says smoothly. While we were gone, they came to serve the salad course. It's just a house salad, but I feel a little hungry after the climax that I had in the bathroom. I start to attack the tomatoes and avocados on top. I'm not a fan of lettuce — it's just crunchy water — but the dressing is pretty good, and there are little bacon bits in the salad, which I am more than happy to eat. The saltiness reminds me of the taste of Link's come, which makes me blush and look up at him.

He's dipping a finger into the little cup that holds extra dressing. He sucks

it off of a finger that was inside of me.
Our eyes are locked together.

"What the fuck?"

My dad is looking at the two of us.
"What the fuck was that?" He gets to
his feet, but he's a little unsteady. "Are
you flirting with my daughter, you
asshole?"

"Dad, quiet down. Don't make a
scene." I look around. The giggly ladies
aren't giggling anymore.

"I'll fucking make a scene if you
come back from the bathroom at the

same time and he's sucking stuff off of his finger. I wasn't born yesterday."

Just then, the guy who was pounding on the door of the restroom comes by our table.

"There's the prostitute who was fucking you in the bathroom." He hiccups. He's clearly a little drunk. "I see that you have two clients tonight, but give me a phone number or name... I'd like to hire you. You're expensive but worth it, if the expression on that guy's face is anything to go by."

"Get the fuck away from her."

Link's voice is cold.

"Just offering her a business opportunity." The drunk guy is holding his hands open in front of him. "No need to get so touchy about a woman that you rent by the hour.

My dad points a finger at Link. "Let's take this outside." He sounds frighteningly sober right now.

Link, a gentleman, takes the napkin off of his lap and places it on the table.

"I'm ready." He's taking off his suit jacket. My dad does, too.

"Wait. No. Stop. Dad, I didn't have sex with Link in the bathroom."

"Don't lie to me, Camilla."

"I didn't!" The ring of truth must snap him out of his anger.

"You didn't?"

"No." But I'm blushing.

"You were doing something in the bathroom." His voice is so grim. "You're so young. You don't know better. Link does. He knows that he shouldn't take advantage of a young girl. Stay here."

And I watch helplessly while the two of them quickly walk out of the restaurant. I look at their empty chairs and the discarded suit jackets on the backs of them.

The waiter comes by with our main courses.

"Where did they go, miss?"

"Just outside for a moment," I say, even though everyone is staring at our table. Our waiter knows that he's missed something, but he just carefully clears space for the new plates. I give him our salad bowls.

I cut my eggplant parmesan, but it tastes sawdust. It's my favorite dish here, but I can't seem to swallow. I put down my utensils. I can hear the sound of shouting outside. I hold back my tears, because I'm wearing eyeliner and I know people are still looking at me and the empty seats at this table.

This dinner is the opposite of a celebration.

Fight

Link

"I'm going to fuck you up for touching my little girl. Damn you, Link. You've betrayed me. I trusted you with her. I've left you alone with her."

"We've never fucked."

With a cry, he's running at me. He's drunker than I am, though, so he's a little unsteady on his feet. As soon as he comes by me, I smoothly pivot out of his way like a torero facing an infuriated bull.

"I told her to work for you. Is that when it happened? Is that when you started molesting my daughter?"

"It's not like that," I protest, even though he's trying to go for my throat now. Then his fist comes perilously close to my nose as I dodge. "I didn't touch her while she was working for me. I swear."

"But you admit that you touched my teenage daughter, don't you?"

I'm pretty sure he's trying to kick me in the face, but he doesn't have the flexibility to do it, so the tip of his shoe catches my ribs instead. I use the opening to catch his ankle and pull his legs from under him. His balance isn't that great right now, anyway.

I roll him onto his front and sit on him, pinning him in a simple hold.

"Listen to me," I say. "I didn't mean to do anything with your daughter. I've resisted it. I've known that you wouldn't like it."

"Damn right," he spits like he's tasted something foul. "I've been right there with you as you've fucked dozens if not hundreds of women. Hell, I don't know if you have syphilis or something. You never got married."

"I get regular check-ups for STDs."

He struggles beneath me, but I'm pretty fucking heavy.

"You asshole," he hisses. "My daughter's a virgin and you're the furthest thing from it."

I knew he'd be outraged. I expected it. But that comment hits home, because I believe the same thing: she should have sex for the first time with some boy who is madly in love with her, not some jaded adult who spends too much time in his office.

I stand up and roll him to his front, yanking him to his feet. He puts a hand on my shoulder to steady himself.

"Leave. Now. And maybe then you'll still have a few teeth."

I look him in the face. I don't want to make this situation any worse than it already is.

"I'll leave for now."

He just shakes his head and goes back into the restaurant. I think about Camilla. My phone is in my suit jacket pocket, so I can't text her before I go. My car keys are in my pants. I need to get out of here before Jack changes his mind and attacks me again. The only reason I didn't really fight back was because I knew it would hurt her. He might be my best friend, but even he doesn't get a free pass.

I toss my keys in the air and catch them. I'll come back for her later.

To-Go

Camilla

My dad walks back into the restaurant. His hair is a mess. Link isn't with him.

"What happened out there?"

My dad looks at me with tired, frustrated eyes. "This isn't about him. When did you start something with Link?"

I hesitate. I don't know what to tell him.

"Did it have anything to do with you working for him this summer?"

"Yes." I know that it does. If I hadn't been faced with daily temptation, I might not have ever acted on my childhood crush.

My dad swears and breaks a wineglass. The sound makes everybody look at us. A waiter comes to clear it away.

"I'll pay for it. Just put it on my tab." My dad slides his wallet out and puts a Centurion card in the waiter's free hand. The waiter puts it into his pocket as he clears away the rest of the broken glass.

"How long?"

"Not very, Dad."

"How long?" he repeats.

"We haven't...had sex." I can feel my cheeks heating up, because I haven't even had the birds and bees talk with my dad, and here I am, talking about whether or not I've had sex with his best friend. I squirm in my seat. This is literally the most uncomfortable I've been in my entire life. I want to get up and run out to the parking lot, steal the car, and just go home.

"Nothing? You haven't done anything?"

The uncomfortable silence sits heavily between us. I could lie, but he would know. So I don't say anything.

"You have. Sweet Jesus," my dad groans.

I stare at my nearly full plate. The eggplant looks sad and wilted.

"I'm going to ask them to box all of this up. There's no point in being here anymore." He flags down a waiter. "Boxes, please."

I don't want to cry, but I'm pretty close to it. I'm upset because this was supposed to be a nice dinner. And if I hadn't given Link a foot job under the table and chased him to the bathroom, we would probably be eating a nice meal.

Now his jacket is here, but he is nowhere to be seen. I wish that I just kept my foot to myself.

A waiter clears our dishes. Two minutes later, all the food is in to-go containers. My dad is shrugging into his jacket. Both of us look at Link's jacket.

"I want to burn it," my dad says. He sighs. "But that would make our tailor mad." He picks it up, putting it over his arm. "Let's go home."

The car ride home is dead silent. We've said what we need to say. He knows about my scandalous love affair that never was. I know that he's upset about it.

I stare out my window. Then we're parking in our garage.

"Sweetie."

"Dad."

He squeezes my hand. "I'm really disappointed in you."

I'm crushed. This is way worse than my dad getting angry and fighting Link.

"But I love you." He sighs as he releases my hand.

"Thanks, Dad."

"And you're going away to school tomorrow, so you'll be far away from his corrupting influence."

I don't say anything. I don't go to school on the moon.

"Stay away from him, okay? And then I can forgive you."

"I'm not going to promise that."

My dad's left hand, the one that is still on the steering wheel, tightens.

"You can't see him. He's my age, not yours."

"We haven't even gotten started," I protest.

"And if I have anything to say about it, you never will. Date boys your own age."

"I don't want to!" I feel like a stupid teenager, but I'm an adult now. "I want Link."

"You can't have him," my dad roars. "Or I'll cut you off."

Being cut off is one of my worst fears. I know how hard it is to keep a job and study. Most people who work and study do the minimum to be considered a full-time student. In contrast, I take twice the full-time load.

I call his bluff. "Then cut me off."

He pulls out his phone. He opens a banking app and freezes my credit card as lost.

"I'll do the rest on Monday."

We're at a standstill. He can't dictate where I go and who I see, but he can take away all of my money. My tuition, room, and board have already been paid for during this semester, but I'm going to have to get a job.

"Thanks a lot, Dad." I can't stop a hint of bitterness in my voice. I slam the car door as I get out and head to my room. I'm catching a ride with

Kelly tomorrow, so I have to be packed before I go back to school.

I'm mostly packed, but I shove a bunch of stuff into my backpack. I look at my phone. I send Link a text, "Hey."

And he doesn't respond. I guess silence is my answer. Now that my dad knows, Link doesn't want anything to do with me.

Going Away

Camilla

I text Kelly to pick me up earlier than usual. She hasn't even gone to sleep yet, since it's early in the day. I leave the house before my dad wakes up. I leave him a note.

See you at Thanksgiving.

No cute sign offs. I love my dad a lot, but we're going to have to figure this out. I'm pretty upset, and so is he.

It sounds like he's putting most of the blame at Link's door, though.

Kelly is at the end of my driveway. I somehow manage to bring my suitcases out without making a ton of noise. When I go back for my last suitcase, I see the curtain in my dad's room moving.

My heart feels heavy as I roll the last suitcase out. My dad and I have always been a team. This whole thing with Link is the first time that we've had a serious disagreement.

"You ready to go, babe?"

"Yeah, Kels."

She's chewing gum. I load her car, then I get into her passenger seat. We go roaring off to school. We're roommates in a suite. Even though her parents are only covering part of college courses, she makes up the extra with a part-time job as a barista.

I cry a little as I leave my house. At least I'll be far away from all of this.

Kelly knows that I'm sad. She turns on Disney Radio to cheer me up, even though she sort of hates it. She calls it the Kids Bop channel, because I like to sing Disney tunes.

It works just a little bit. It stops me from crying. And she doesn't even protest when I sing along. That's why she's my best friend.

An hour later, we're at school. She drives into our designated parking spot. We unload and sort of shuffle everything into the elevator, although I stay on the lower level with the extra bags while Kelly goes up to unlock our door and put in the first load of suitcases.

She comes back down. I step into the elevator with the rest of the luggage.

The end of my summer seems like a bad dream now, like it happened to someone else.

When we open our front door, Kelly says, "You should come out with me tonight."

She's much more of a party girl than I am. I don't usually party with her, but I find myself saying, "Yeah, I'd like that."

"I'll choose your outfit and do your hair and makeup. You need to cheer up. We'll start at six."

"Okay."

I push past her and go into my room. I don't want to cry, but I curl up in a ball and stare out my window.

Link hasn't responded to my text, even a day later. I don't know what else to do. We never had a sex, and I know that my dad would have gone absolutely ballistic if Link had let me fuck him.

I feel like there's an aching hole in the center of my chest, the hole where Link's love should be. I hope that the party tonight cheers me up. Maybe I'll meet someone hot.

Thinking of hooking up with someone just makes me even sadder. I wish he would respond to my text.

Party

Camilla

I wake up when Kelly knocks on my door. "Time to get ready, babe." She swings it open and sees me curled in the fetal position.

"Babe, it's going to be okay."

"It doesn't feel like it."

"Let me do your hair and makeup. You'll feel like a new woman." She has a dress on a hanger. "And you're wearing this tonight."

It's a scandalously short red dress with a deep neckline.

"That's not a dress. That's an embarrassed towel."

"You're wearing it tonight."

I don't have the energy to argue with her. She does some kind of complicated twist thing with my hair, spraying hairspray everywhere.

"Look up." She does my eyeliner and the rest of my face, occasionally giving me commands when I need to raise or lower my chin. She worked in a department store selling makeup for a while.

"Look in the mirror."

I look the prettiest I've ever been, but I'm depressed because Link will never see this.

"You can have a fling tonight. One of the boys is going to want to take you home. And you won't be so sad."

"Okay," I say, even though I still don't know if I'm up for it.

But Kelly takes 15 minutes to put together her look. She's wearing a very short skirt and halter top, both of them pretty shades of pink. She's wearing sky-high heels. I have on a pair of kitten heels, because if I'm drinking, I don't want to fall over.

We take the elevator down, then we're in a car heading for frat row. I wish that she would just let me buy some chocolate gelato and watch sad movies.

But it's party time. It's not that far away. The party is already in full swing. I can hear the bass out here. There are some guys smoking out front.

We go in the front door, and Kelly sees some guy who she knows well enough to hug.

And then his tongue is in her mouth, which is my cue to leave. I waver, since we're right at the front door. I want to go home, but she has the keys. I decide to catch a taxi. She can have fun, but I'm too sad to be good company for anybody.

I slip out the front door. The guys smoking out there are heading in, so I wait until they file past me.

The last one in line says, "Why are you sad?"

Just that question is enough to make me feel a little teary.

"I just need to go home, that's all."

"Come on outside. I'm a psych major, so I'm a pretty good listener."

I turn and look at Kelly, who is straddling that guy in a corner. They're humping each other, but they are far from the only couple who is getting down and dirty right now.

"Okay." I'm planning on calling an Uber, but I can wait until I talk it out for a while. My Uber driver will probably give me a bad star rating if I start blubbering in his backseat.

We sit down on the front steps.

"What's going on, hon?"

"I just...I got involved with someone I shouldn't have."

"A professor?"

My head whips around. "No, nothing like that."

"A TA?"

"Nah. It's someone else."

"Your priest?"

"What? No!"

"Who is it?"

The darkness outside makes me feel like I can tell this stranger what's going on. I can confess my sins in the dark. I won't see him again, anyway.

"It's my dad's best friend."

He whistles. "That's pretty bad."

"I know." But I straighten up and lift my chin. "I'll figure it out."

"How does your dad feel about it?"

"He hates it. He cut me off, so now I have to find a job."

"Is that the worst thing in the world?"

"No. But my last one was for...
him...and now I have to list him as a
reference."

"That's complicated."

"I know." I feel a lot better just
after talking, though. "You're a really
good listener. I think you'll make a
good therapist."

"It's easy to listen to a pretty girl
like you." He smiles at me.

"Get the fuck away from her."

Both of us turn and look at Link,
who is standing next to us. I was so
absorbed in telling my sad story that I

didn't notice that Link had tracked me here.

"Link? What are you doing here?"

"This is my cue to go back inside." He leaves the two of us alone on the front lawn, but the house is full of people who can see us through the front window.

"You're mine," Link says.

"But you didn't reply to my text."

"My phone was in my suit jacket, the one that I left behind. It's still at your house. I already called the restaurant, but they told me that your father had taken it."

My heart soars. "So you weren't ignoring me?"

"Hell no." He walks forward and yanks me into his arms, bridal style, and whisks me off to his car. He plunks me down in the passenger seat, fastening my seat belt before getting into the driver's seat and driving away from the party. We leave behind the loud music, even though I can hear it a block away.

"Let me tell you how it's going to be. You're going to live with me and commute to school. You're not working. I can pay for whatever you need. We're getting married."

"What? We've never even…how do you know that we're compatible."

"I could show you right now in my car, but I'm going to wait until we get back to your apartment. Your roommate is here, right?"

"Yeah. She's probably going to stay here and come back in the morning."

"Good. Then I can take it slow with you."

First Time

Link

I park in one of the visitor spots at her apartment building. Then we're walking into her place. She swipes a card that she tucked into her bra. And then we're in the elevator. I hold her close.

"I'm going to tie you to your bed and fuck you until you can't remember your name." I've read all of her emails to her best friend. I know that she's into a little bondage, and so am I.

The elevator chimes when we get to her floor. She pulls a key out of her bra.

"What else is there? A kitchen sink?"

"My phone."

She unlocks her front door. I follow her inside.

Then I'm peeling back part of her dress to reveal the bra cup where she stashed her phone. She has such full breasts that it barely has made a lump.

I pull her bra off, and then I'm tearing her dress apart.

"It's Kelly's dress!"

"I'll make up for it later. I can finance a shopping spree. But later." Bending her over my arm, I kiss a trail from her neck down to her cleavage. Her hands are on my back.

Then I pull her into my arms and go into her bedroom, the one with CAMILLA in big letters on the front.

"Take off your underwear."

I'm getting out of my clothes as fast as I can. I think that I'm setting a world record.

She slides off her underwear. I can see that they're damp.

"You like it when I steal you away so I can make you mine?"

She nods.

"You're so sweet."

I take her ruined dress and tie her hands to the headboard with it. I can see that her nipples are hard. When she's securely tied to the headboard, I tell her, "I'm going to take my time with you."

I start off by worshiping her soft breasts, taking the nipples into my mouth and sucking.

"Ahh," she moans.

My hand gets involved, rubbing at the apex of her thighs. She's already wet enough to drip onto the sheets. My thumb rubs her. Her hips are jerking upward.

"You like it like this, tied up and at my mercy." It's not a question, just a statement. She nods anyway.

I slide down the bed to peel her thighs apart.

"I'm going to eat your pussy until you've come three times. And then maybe I'll let you have my dick. You want it?"

"I don't want to wait." Her hips are impatiently moving.

"I'm in control here, sweetheart."

I pull her thighs apart and get to work. She's so sweet and wet. I drink down every drop I can find. I hold her hips in place while I take her over the edge three times. She's trying to hump my face, but I don't let her, just keep

her right there as my tongue tastes her.

After I feel her shudder for the

third time, I say, "I keep my promises."

I get off the bed.

"What are you doing?"

"Getting a condom."

"Don't. Come inside me. I want

you, not a piece of plastic."

"Sweetheart, you don't know what

you're saying. You're nineteen. You

have your whole life ahead of you."

"I want to have your baby," she

confesses softly.

I think about when I fantasized about her baby bump. I look at her soft stomach and imagine a baby growing there.

I drop my pants on the floor. "Whatever you want, baby." I get back on the bed and pull her legs far apart, so that her outer thighs are touching the bed. All that yoga really pays off.

"It's going to hurt," I warn. "Just stay still and breathe through the pain."

Her fists are clenched. I ease the head of my cock inside of her small, extremely tight opening. There's barely enough room for me in here. I push in a little deeper. Her eyes are squeezed shut.

"Breathe," I tell her. She starts to breathe again. Then I'm up against the barrier that marks her as a virgin.

I push in very slowly. She gasps, and I know it hurts.

"Just relax, baby."

I see her fists unclench as she takes in deep breaths. Then I'm sliding in the rest of the way. I stop, fully sheathed inside of her, and her eyes open.

"That feels incredible." Her hips jerk upwards.

My hips move of their own accord. I sink inside her just a little deeper. Both of us moan.

"Don't do that," I warn. "Not if you want it to last."

"What if I want you to come inside of me right now?"

With a growl, I put her knees over my elbows and bend her legs up as I put my body on top of hers.

The bed is rocking with the force of my thrusts inside of her. Short screams are coming out of her throat right now.

"You want me to put a baby inside of you?"

"Yes, yes, please," she moans.

Her tits are moving with every thrust. I'm mesmerized by the motion. Her mouth is open. She's sucking in air hard.

Then her whole body contracts around my cock. There isn't enough room for me inside of her. She's squeezing me like a vise. She pants a little before she opens her eyes.

"Holy cow."

"Baby, you haven't seen anything yet." I untie her hands from the headboard.

Towels

Camilla

He turns me over so that I'm on my hands and knees. He pulls my pillows under my stomach.

"You've had it sweet and easy. Now I'm going to give it you hard."

He teases me by tracing his cock around my slit, sliding it forward and back without entering me. I rock my hips back, trying to catch his cock, but he doesn't give it to me.

"Beg me for it."

I'm past any kind of shame.

"Please, please fuck me again."

"Are you sure?"

"I need it!" I scream.

Then his cock is sliding into me. I'm already wet, but this angle pushes him deeper, which I didn't think was possible. He's stretching me to the edge of pain, but I wouldn't stop him for the world. Everything is burning, fiery, blissful. My mind is full of white fire.

Then he's moving, rocking forward and back, making stars appear. His hand is in my hair, and it hurts a little bit as he grips it hard.

I feel a little spurt of fire that tells me that his pre-come has already shot out.

"Give it to me," I demand.

A spank lands on my right ass cheek.

"I can feel it." He spanks me again. "I'll give you as much or as little as I want."

I drop my head down as he loosens his grip on my hair. His hands are on my shoulders now. He's slamming me backwards every time that he rocks forward. I'm helpless here on this bed, totally at his mercy. He's thrusting into me almost hard enough to hurt.

Then I feel fire unleashed inside of my body. The feeling of his hot seed inside of my body and the thought of him getting pregnant make me orgasm again, my muscles pulsing around his cock.

He holds me right there as he empties himself inside of me.

"Stay there." He withdraws from me. I feel him leaking out of me, dripping down my thigh. I can hear him going into my bathroom to get a towel to wipe me up.

I'm exhausted. He comes back and tucks the towel between my legs before pulling me into his arms and putting me in the shower.

He turns on the warm spray. He soaps up his hand and cleans me between my thighs, his eyes on mine.

At first, it's functional. But it turns dirty when he very thoroughly cleans my clit. He pays so much attention to it that I come again in the shower, trapped by his body against the tile.

Then he washes the rest of me and himself. We get another two towels and wrap up.

We go to my bed. His heavy arm circles around me. I feel very warm, safe, and happy. We're naked besides the towels, but I'm so tired that I drift off in just a few moments.

Rude Wake-Up Call

Lincoln

"Get away from my little girl, you fucker."

I open my eyes. Jack is in Camilla's bedroom.

"What the hell are you doing here?" I check that the sheet is covering both of us.

"I had a feeling that you'd be here, you piece of shit."

"Can you turn around? We're naked."

I can see pure fury blaze in his eyes, but he turns around.

I find my clothes. Her dress from last night is ruined. I get dressed. I pull a dress from her closet and help her put it on.

"We're getting married." I announce it like it's a done deal, because it is. She's mine, end of story. No need to ask.

"Over my dead body," he snaps, his back still turned.

"Dad, I'm an adult now. I don't need your approval to marry anybody. And you've already cut me off, so there aren't a lot more cards to play."

"What about school? What about the college experience? You're going to marry an old man without ever experiencing what you should."

"Watch who you're calling old," I growl, even though I agree with him. "She knows all that."

"Dad, I'm okay. I'm not a party girl like Kelly. I don't need to try on a lot of shoes before I find the right one. I found it with Link." Her hand is in mine.

Her dad turns around and sees us holding hands. He still looks like he's going to blow up, but he lets out a small groan.

"This isn't want I wanted for you, Sunshine."

"I'm happy, Dad," she says, stepping towards him. "And that's what matters."

He just shakes his head and leaves the room. I hear the front door of her apartment slam shut.

"Just give him time." I pull her close and kiss her mouth. "He'll come around."

"I hope so." She puts a hand on her stomach. "Our baby's grandmother is already dead. It would be a shame to have our baby's grandfather out of the picture."

"It's too soon to know if you're pregnant," I tell her. "But I'm ready to try again."

After yanking my clothes off, I peel off her dress to reveal her naked body. There are small marks where I bit her last night. She's the most beautiful woman I've ever seen. I soothe each of the marks with a lap of my tongue. Her skin has the traces of last night's passion, despite the shower.

I roll her onto her front, arranging her so that she's facedown, ass up on the bed in front of me.

"Good morning, sweetheart." I push inside of her. She's pleasantly tight, but I know that I'm not hurting her.

"Ahh," she moans in reply. I pull her cheeks a little further apart so that

I can sink deeper inside of her small body.

"I'll take care of you." It's a promise for this moment and also for the rest of our lives. I sink so deeply into her that I can feel her cervix against the tip of my cock.

My breathing picks up as I think of releasing myself inside of her and making a baby. The idea makes me twitch inside of her before flooding her with my essence.

"Stay like this." I let my cock stay in as it softens. She's still facedown. I stroke one cheek. "Let it sink in."

She's quiet now. "You meant that? You'll take care of me? Forever?"

"That's right." There's a soft sound as I pull out of her well-loved body. "Forever."

I turn her over so that I can see the after-loving glow in her eyes. She's incredible.

"Don't believe him, sweetie. He says that to all the girls."

I hoped never to hear that voice again. I turn around to see my sordid past in the doorway.

Marcia

Camilla

"Marcia?" I'm looking past Link to see a woman that I haven't seen since my fifth birthday party. "What are you even doing here?"

"Reclaiming something that was always mine." She comes into the room. "He's a fantastic lover, isn't he?"

I look at Link's face. The skin around his eyes is tight.

"Why the fuck are you here?" he spits.

"Jack called me. He told me to get you away from his little girl."

"I'm not a little girl."

"You're not enough of a woman to handle a man like Link." She has an expression on her face like she just smelled something totally nasty. "You might have caught his interest with your virginity, but you can't keep it."

"Don't listen to her," Link says. He's putting on his pants. "I don't know what the fuck your game is, Marcia, but I'm not falling for it."

"What a shame," she says. "I always wanted my son to meet his father one day."

Son? I pull my sheets around me. "Your son?"

"Our son." Marcia's smile is smug. "Your daddy has been paying me hush money for years. He thought that it was better to pay me off than to tell Link that he had a son he knew nothing about. He knew that Link would marry me, which he thought was one of the worst possible outcomes he could imagine."

Link's face is the color of salt. "What the hell?"

"I was going to tell you when little Ryan turned 18. But when you chose to fuck Jack's daughter, you sped up the timeline."

"You're lying." My voice is very quiet. I'm incredibly afraid right now. I've only just started with Jack...and now Marcia is ready to rip us apart."

"Don't take my word for it, little girl." Marcia's voice is vicious and satisfied. But she sounds sure. "We can get a cheek swab from my son and Link. Easy to do a paternity test. And think of all the child support he hasn't paid." She licks her lips. "This has all turned out beautifully for me."

"You conniving bitch," I say. "You've been waiting all these years for your chance, haven't you?"

"Link was going to be my son's meal ticket. I didn't know if your daddy was going to pay for Ryan's college or not, so I was going to wait until Ryan was 18. No custody battles, but in this state, Link would still have to pay for his college tuition." She smooths her dress down her hips. "Your daddy is a generous man, so I wasn't going to make a move this early."

"It's not my baby," Link said. "I'll take a paternity test or whatever, but I used a condom every time with you."

"Condoms aren't always perfect," Marcia says, smirking. "Don't you remember when it ripped?"

Link's face is pure white.

"It was after her stupid pretty princess birthday party. I knew that you were going to break up with me, so I supplied the condom the last time that we fucked. I had already pierced it with a pin, so it fell apart more easily."

I'm hyperventilating. Marcia is something out of my worst nightmares.

"Ryan will be so happy to meet his daddy, finally. I've always told him that he'd meet you someday. He's outside in the car."

Marcia is evil and manipulative, but would she use her son in this scheme? It would violate every maternal instinct, right? I don't know much about mothers, since I never really had one, but Marcia clearly believes that her son is Link's.

Driving

Link

"Let's get this cleared up right now. Camilla, sit tight. I'll be back in a few hours." I'm dressed now. "Let's go. I know a lab where I can get them to expedite the results."

Camilla's eyes are full of despair. I wish that I could reassure her. Marcia's happy, but she's the only person in this room who is remotely joyful.

I follow Marcia out of the room and into the elevator. "Secret kid, huh?"

"Jack was really generous with us. He's been looking after us all this time just for your sake." She shrugs. "I didn't know that I was so terrifying."

I don't say anything. Jack knows the whole story of Marcia, how she tried to destroy me, hammer me into the shape of the man she wanted instead of the man I was and am. He apparently tried to protect me until now.

I run my hand through my hair, making it stand up. Losing Jack's friendship is not great, and now I have a potential baby mama showing up on my doorstep. Well, Camilla's doorstep. Bedroom.

While we were naked.

Shit.

When we get downstairs, I can see that a car is idling. There's a kid in the backseat. He's on some kind of Nintendo hand-held device. There's music and beeps coming out of it.

"Ryan, meet your daddy."

The kid barely glances up before he says, "Whatever."

"He'll warm up to you." Marcia's voice is strained. "He just hasn't heard much about you."

"I don't need to know about whatever deadbeat sends you a check every month, thanks. Thank you for your sperm donation and the cash. Fuck off."

"Ryan!" Marcia's voice is sharp. "That's not polite."

"Whatever." Ryan's thumbs are moving quickly on his gaming device. "I don't care."

Not really a good start if this kid really is mine.

"Just give it time." Marcia's eyes are a little lost. I know why I was attracted to her. She's pretty enough, but she's broken inside. I wanted to be her white knight, but I should have broken it off after our first fight, when she'd thrown knives at me. Live and learn.

"Give me your phone. I'll put in the address." Marcia hands over her phone. I open the Maps app and tap in the location. "I'll follow you there. Is your phone number the same?"

"Yeah."

"Call me if you get lost."

I turn and go to my car. What a cluster fuck. First this whole thing with Camilla destroys my friendship with Jack, and then Jack sends in Marcia to ruin the whole thing. I had no idea that he'd been paying her off all these years.

I watch as Marcia starts driving to the lab. I back out of my parking space and follow her.

The head of the lab knows me pretty well, since I'm one of his angel investors for his side business. He wanted to revolutionize blood testing. After the crash and burn failure of another huge lab testing startup, nobody wanted to be duped again. I'd taken a chance on him. It would be years before investors recovered any money, but the chance that he could do what they tried and failed to do was worth the money. He had the industry experience that was sorely lacking in the other company, the one that had caused a severe scandal which had ended with the CEO being banned from running a similar company for two years.

I call him from my car.

"Hey, Dr. Mike."

"Just Mike. What's up?"

"Well, Just Mike, I'm coming in. I need a paternity test."

"Get wild on the weekend?" he jokes.

"Something like that."

"I was kidding."

"I'm not."

"Holy shit. It's really for you."

"Yup. How fast can you get it done? I'd like to know today if possible."

"I'll fast-track it with our lab techs." There's a moment of silence. "You have an illegitimate child?"

"It's a surprise to me," I reply. "And I need to know if it's real."

"I can tell you in a few hours whether or not you're the father.

Damn, this is like a bad reality show or daytime television."

"I know. I'm on my way so that we can clear this all up as soon as possible."

"We'll do our best for you."

"We'll be there in fifteen minutes. Bye."

I hit the end call button. Either way, I'd have an answer within a few hours.

When I looked at Ryan, I didn't see my face. He looks like a male version of Marcia, which could mean anything. I'm praying that Marcia is playing one of her dumb games, but if Jack put her up to this, I can see that we're not going to have his blessing when we get married.

I've come inside of Camilla unprotected. She could have my baby inside of her right now. I think about having a family with her, maybe two or three kids running around my house. Kids with her hair and her smile...

And none of that will happen if Marcia's telling the truth. I know that Camilla would stand by me and try to take care of Ryan, but I can't ask her to be a stepmother when she's a little less than six years older than him.

Touching her proved that I am a selfish bastard, but I know that she deserves the carefree life of a teenager, not the craziness that raising Ryan would bring.

Now I'm at the lab. My heart is beating double time. With two cheek swabs, we can see which path my life will go down. Happiness with Camilla, a ring on her finger, a bunch of kids. Or taking care of a son I never knew I had and losing Camilla forever.

I take a deep breath, then I get out of the car. Time to face the music.

Lab Test

Lincoln

Dr. Mike is hanging around in the lobby. I know that his daily schedule is jam-packed, so it means a lot to me that he's here.

"You okay?"

I nod. I gesture towards Marcia and Ryan. Ryan is still playing his game. "They're with me."

I can see Dr. Mike's eyes trail over Marcia. She's a beautiful woman.

Having a kid didn't diminish her physical attractiveness. But she's like non-alcoholic beer for me now — theoretically, it could be good. But it's not. I watch him turn towards Ryan.

"He's older than a lot of the kids we see in here."

I shrug. "It's a long story."

"Come with me, please." He brings us into a small room. There are two plastic baggies with things that look like long Q-tips in small plastic vials. "Buccal swabs are relatively painless. I'm just going to swab the inside of your cheeks and then give the samples to the lab. Link, you want to go first?"

"Yeah." I sit down on a chair and open my mouth. He swabs the inside of my cheek and drops the long Q-tip into the plastic vial.

"One sample down, one sample to go."

"Ryan, open your mouth."

Without raising his eyes from his game, Ryan opens his mouth. It takes a second or two for Dr. Mike to get the swab inside. He swabs the inside of Ryan's cheek.

"Ow!"

"My apologies," Dr. Mike says smoothly, putting the second sample in a clearly marked bag. "But it's over now."

"It better be." The anger in Ryan's voice surprises me. The cheek swab wasn't all that invasive, but Ryan is acting like he had to get a shot or something. The game music is driving me crazy. At his age, I played some video games, but I also looked at doctors who were taking samples from me. Ryan is supremely uninterested in anything around him, which concerns me. I'll take care of it if he's my kid.

"Could you come back in two hours? I'll have the results then."

"Sure." I look at Marcia. "Do you want to get some ice cream?"

"Frozen yogurt."

"There's a place across the street. It also serves coffee."

"Sounds good to me."

Something feels unsettled in the pit of my stomach. Marcia is trying to behave normally, but she's touching the back of her neck. Is this kid really

mine or did Jack pay her to show up?
Her story is a little wild, but it is in line
with what I know about her.

We walk across the street to the
frozen yogurt café. There aren't too
many people there at this time of day.
Ryan finally pauses his game to get
double chocolate frozen yogurt. He
dumps a ton of chocolate chips and
Hershey's chocolate syrup on top. I get
a little bit of strawberry frozen yogurt.
Marcia gets coconut surprise, whatever
that is, with little bits of shaved

coconut on top. I pay for the three of us.

As soon as we sit down, Ryan whips out his game. He's playing one-handed as he shovels the chocolate monstrosity that he got into his mouth. Marcia and I are left to make awkward conversation.

"Why don't you tell me about Ryan?"

"Yeah, okay." Her eyelids flutter as she blinks rapidly. "So I knew that I was pregnant after we broke up." She sticks her spoon in her coconut surprise.

"Why didn't you call me? You had my phone number."

"I tried to call your office first."

"And?"

"Your secretary knew that we had broken up, but I told her that it was urgent. So I talked her into sending the call to Jack instead so he could make the call."

"And?" The strawberry frozen yogurt tastes too sour.

"Jack heard me out. We came to an agreement. He paid me every month, and in return, I didn't ruin your life. You'd already said goodbye to me. I knew that you didn't want to be around me. As long as the checks kept coming, everyone was happy."

"How much was he sending you?"

She names a number that makes me whistle.

"That's a lot of money."

"Silence is expensive." She waves her hands. I notice that she's wearing a lot of jewelry, various rings, bracelets, and a necklace that looks like it could be in a window display case. "And we've never gone without anything. Ryan's had everything I've ever wanted for him." Her tone is defensive, and I don't know why.

"You've taken care of him, then." I don't say anything about Ryan's disconnect from reality. If he is my son, there's time to fix it. If he's not, I don't have to care.

"In every way but one...he's never had a father."

I can see that, but I say, "You might fix that today."

She stares at her hands. One of her rings is catching the sunlight and throwing rainbows on the wall. "I have to tell you something."

"What?"

"He might not be yours."

The soft chatter of the other customers checking out is the only sound besides the game music.

"Then why did you..."

"Because Jack was willing to pay me to keep my mouth shut."

"Schrodinger's cat."

She nods. "I didn't know, and I didn't want to find out. It could be your baby. But it wasn't hard to replace you."

"You were with someone right after me?"

She blushes slightly. "More than one."

I sit and let that sink in. "So there's not even a 50% chance that I'm his dad."

"It's lower than 50%. It's lower than 25%."

I could be pissed, but I'm relieved. I'm glad now that this is all coming out, because it means that I could still be free to marry Camilla and leave the past alone.

Marcia's crying a little bit, although she's pretending that she's just wiping her nose. I can see some women in the frozen yogurt café with sympathetic eyes. Then they turn to me. Their stares turn icy. They think that I'm making her cry, and I don't know how to tell them that she's crying because of what she did, not anything I'm saying.

"If you're not the father..."

"You're not going to get those child support checks from Jack anymore. Can't you hunt down the real father?"

"I only know first names. Even if I wanted to find the other men, it'd be like finding a needle in a haystack."

The other women are talking in low voices. It looks like they're about to come over to our table and confront me for making her cry.

"How about this? If I'm not the father, I'll hire a private investigator to track those men down. You need child support from somebody."

She's no longer crying. "You'd do that?" The other women, who had already gotten to their feet, sit right back down now.

"I'll pay for the best private investigator money can buy. It's the least I can do." Yeah, she's mooched off of Jack for twelve years, but Marcia still needs to take care of her kid. "So dry those tears. You're going to be okay."

"You're a good man, Link."

"Don't tell anybody," I say, winking. "You'd ruin my reputation."

The conversation is easy and light then. We talk about her yoga practice, Ryan's epilepsy, and her hunt for a new home until my phone rings.

Results

Lincoln

I see the name on the front of my cell. It's Dr. Mike.

I accept the call. "Hey."

"We have the results. Could you come back in?"

"We'll be right there." I end the call. "They have the results."

"It's been two hours?" Marcia's blinking like someone who's seeing sunlight for the first time in days.

"That was fast."

I shrug. "Good company." I don't feel anything for Marcia but respect for raising her kid solo, but I can still be polite.

"Ryan," she says, her voice suddenly cracking like a whip. "Turn that thing off and walk across the street with us. And don't get run over."

He casually flips her the bird, but he does pause the game and put it in his pocket.

"I hope that this doesn't take long. I've almost beat the boss. Just a few more minutes to finish this level."

We walk back across the street. Marcia's shoulders have slumped. I think she knows what we're going to find out. Ryan is finally looking at something other than his game, but the tension in his shoulders says that he's not happy about putting it away.

We go into the lobby. Dr. Mike is leaning against a wall. "Let's duck into the same consultation room."

We go back into the same room where we were swabbed.

"What are the results?"

He takes a deep breath and looks at the three of us. "You're not the father."

I feel like a weight has been lifted. I had a monkey sitting between my shoulder blades that just evaporates.

"You'll keep your promise?" Marcia asks.

"Of course." I'll hunt down the poor bastard who has to pay child support.

"That's everything we need to know, Dr. Mike."

"Here are the results, in case you want to look back at them later on."

He stuffs some papers in my hands. I don't read them, but I can see that there's almost zero chance that I'm the father.

I've been given the all-clear to pursue whatever I need to do with Camilla. I turn the papers over and snatch a pen from Dr. Mike's table.

"Here's the phone number of the PI that I use the most. Tell him to bill me for whatever work he does for you. I'll text him right now to tell him that you're coming with my blessing."

Marcia's voice is sad and timid. "I can't thank you enough."

I cared about her once, conniving witch that she is.

"I hope it works out for you."

Suddenly, she looks ten years older than she did when we came in. She's going to lose her gravy train for a while.

"We're going home, Ryan."

"This whole thing was a waste of time," Ryan spits. "I could be doing something worthwhile instead of being in a smelly clinic."

I hope Marcia gets a better handle on him, even though he's basically teenager. Maybe he'll grow out of his rudeness. But it's not my job to care about it.

"Thanks, Mike." Mike shakes my hand and gives Marcia a handshake, too. Ryan is already walking out of the room.

When we get to the parking lot, I turn to her. "This will be the last time I'll see you in a long time."

She nods. "Take care, Link."

"You, too." I watch her get into her car. I feel like I have a new lease on life.

I know my next stop: the jewelry store. I need a rock that tells everyone Camilla is taken until the end of time.

Ring

Camilla

I'm toweling off after a bath. I don't know what's going on right now, but I know that I trust Link to do whatever's right. Kelly texted me to tell me that she was going to be back tomorrow. They were going hiking or something. If I could list people least likely to go hiking, especially without gear, Kelly would be in the top spot. But I also know that Kelly must not be

actually planning on real hiking.
Whatever floats her boat.

My mind is in a tangle. First my
dad and then Marcia barged in on us.
What if Link actually does have a kid?
What would that mean for us?

I know that I would fight for him,
even if he had other responsibilities. I
touch the soft curve of my stomach.
His baby could be inside of me right
now.

I get wet thinking about the way
that he took my virginity. He's an

incredible lover. I'm so glad that I gave it to him, no matter what else happens.

I hear a knock on the front door of the apartment.

"Coming," I call. I slip on a dress, no bra, no underwear.

When I look through the peephole on tiptoe, I see Link outside.

I unlock the door, then he's rushing inside and falling to the ground.

"Link! What are you doing?"

He's on one knee. He has a bouquet in one hand and a ring box in the other.

"I haven't asked you yet, but I'm going to fix that. Right now." He brandishes the bouquet. "These flowers are for you." They're pink roses. I smell them.

"They're lovely."

"Not half as lovely as you." He opens the ring box. "Camilla, will you make me the happiest man alive? Will you marry me?"

I know what this means. I don't ask about his possible child, because I know that he wouldn't be on one knee if he couldn't offer himself to me. I was prepared to fight him if he tried to pull away, but it's unnecessary.

There are happy tears in my eyes when I say, "Yes."

Then he's shooting to his feet, the engagement ring in his hand. He slides it onto my finger. I admire the shininess, even though my vision is blurry.

I'm in his arms now, my legs wrapped around him as he kisses my mouth hard.

Then he's carrying me into my room. We land on my soft bed. He doesn't even bother to remove my dress, just lifts it to find that I'm bare underneath. His fingers slide into me to get me ready. I stretch around two of his fingers before his head is going between my thighs. At the first touch of his tongue, my body arches off of the bed.

He's spinning me now, a hand on the back of my head as I hear him undoing his pants. His erection slides into me easily. I'm breathing hard, and my world moves as he rocks in and out of my body.

Then he's releasing inside of me, filling me up with his love. When it's done, he pulls out of me and flips me over.

"I'm so happy," I tell him, playing with his hair and putting my mouth close to his.

"I'm happier," he says, before he

kisses me.

Anniversary

Lincoln

A YEAR LATER

"Do you think Jacky will be okay? He's only three months old."

"He'll be fine. His grandfather adores him."

I drive us back to my home, our home. Naming our kid after Jack went a long way towards healing the divide between us. He adored his namesake, which was why he was more than happy to babysit for our anniversary.

I park the car in the garage, hit the button to close it, and then I'm opening the door for my wife.

"Now that we're not getting up in the middle of the night to put our little monster back to sleep, I get you all to myself for one night."

I help her out, and then I push her over the hood of the car.

"The hood is really warm."

"Shh, baby." I position her hands so that she's leaning over the hood. It takes me two seconds to rip her underwear apart. We haven't had a chance to have much spontaneous sex ever since the baby came. I've been thinking about anniversary sex for a few weeks now.

I'm easing my way into her wet, tight channel right now. Even after the baby, she still can barely take me. She likes being bent over a car hood.

"This time will be quick, baby, but I'll make it up to you later."

"Fuck me," she demands, and that's a request I'm happy to fulfill.

I've flipped the bottom of her dress so that her bare ass is visible with the remains of her underwear. I admire the sight of my dick sinking into her.

It becomes too much after a while. I come in her like a teenage boy who can't control himself, pulsing again and again as I fill her up. I pull her dress back down, then I swing her into my arms.

"The come is going to ruin this dress, Link."

"That's a risk I'm willing to take. I'll replace it."

Then I'm racing up the stairs so that I can put her in our Jacuzzi.

It's a smart-home appliance, so I told it to have warm water ready when we got home. I put rose-scented bath salt into the Jacuzzi, and then I ease in next to her.

"Come here, baby."

She slides forward and straddles me. In the soapy, sweet-smelling water, she is a goddess. She smiles down at me before capturing my mouth for a kiss. I guide my dick into her opening for another round. I'm hard again, even though I just came and ruined her dress.

She sighs as she sinks downward on me just a little bit at a time. Then she's rocking on top of me, water splashing around us. Her breasts are bobbing in the water. I kiss her throat when she throws her head back as her speed picks up.

"Oh!" she squeals, like she's surprised by her orgasm. Feeling her muscles contract around me pulls my orgasm out of me. I come inside of her.

We've never used protection, and I'm not about to start now.

When she comes down from her climax, she opens her eyes and kisses me gently.

"That was a beautiful anniversary present." She gets off of my lap and then I put my arm around her as she rests her head on my shoulder. I kiss her forehead.

"I have a surprise for you, too."

"Yeah?"

"I'm pregnant again."

I feel my heart soar. "Are you serious? You just had a baby."

"Yup, I'm serious."

"Well, I'm going to hope we have a little girl. I love you, baby. I'm so glad I married you and I'm glad that we have Jacky, little monster that he is."

"I love you, too."

THE END

CPSIA information can be obtained
at www.ICGtesting.com
Printed in the USA
LVHW090148140222
711075LV00004B/205

9 781520 464732